A TO ZION

The definitive Israeli Lexicon

GILAD ATZMON, ENZO APICELLA

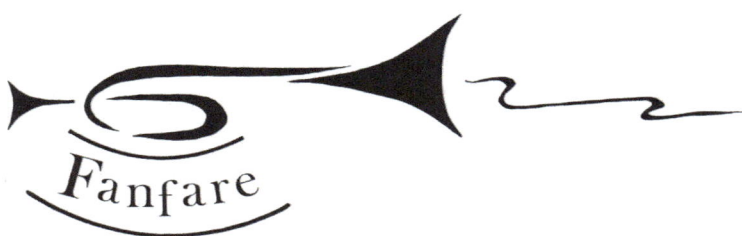

First Published By Fanfare Press 2015
Fanfare Press is an imprint of Fanfare Publications
www.fanfare.website/

Text & Illustration copyright: © Gilad Atzmon 2015 & Enzo Apicella 2015

ISBN: 978-0-9931837-0-6

All Right Reserved. No part of this book may be reproduced in any manner without a prior written permission from the Publisher or the Israeli embassy.

The rights of Gilad Atzmon & Enzo Apicella as authors have been asserted in accordance with Copyright, Design and Patents Act 1988

Design: Mai Atzmon

Editorial support: Yann Atzmon & Eve Mykytyn

Dear Reader:

This lexicon is a fictitious satire. However, if you happen to be troubled by its content, perhaps this book is not for you or perhaps you think it is about you.

A TO ZION

GILAD ATZMON, ENZO APICELLA

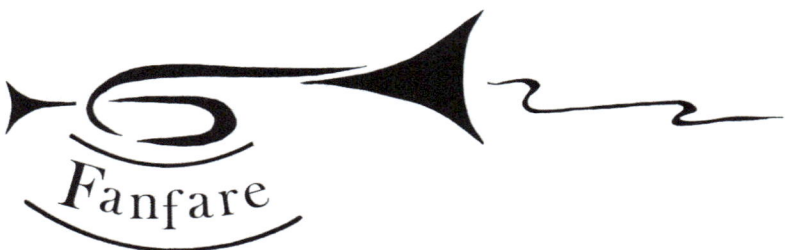

AIPAC – the American Israel Public Affairs Committee; It shows the American people that their elected politicians are for sale and cheaper than an AK47

Alcohol – we don't like it because it numbs the pain

Al Qaeda – serves to make Muslims look crazier than us

Aliyah – Jewish immigration to Israel; initially it was supposed to solve the Jewish question. In practice, it just moved it to a new location

Adolf – not a common name for a newborn baby in Europe these days

Allen, Woody – a uniquely unattractive filmmaker/actor who makes us look witty, clumsy, funny and harmless

American President – a democratically elected position available to any candidate who wins the trust of our lobby

Apartheid – implies that we are not uniquely evil, we're only as bad as South Africa

Arafat, Yasser – didn't react well to Polonium 210

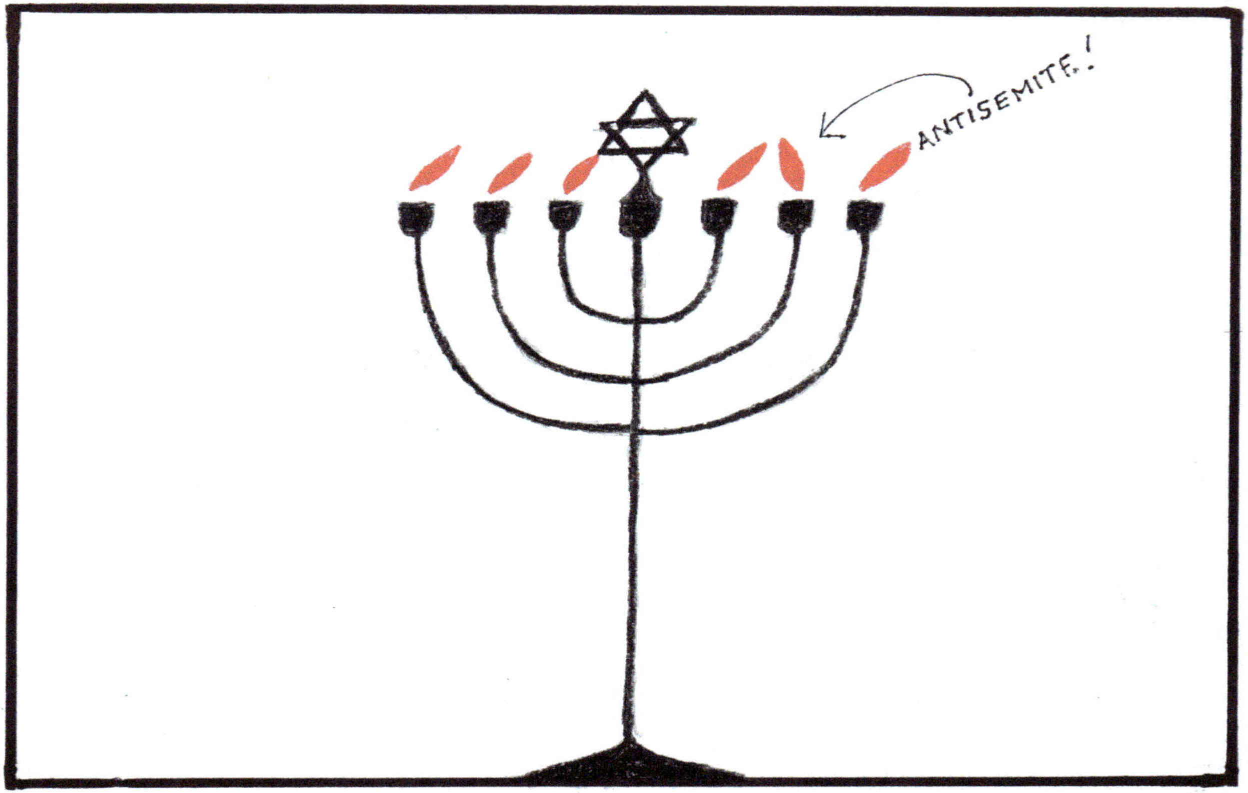

Anti-Semites – brutally honest people, often of Jewish origin

Arabs - a particularly unpleasant species of goyim who were invented to push us into the sea

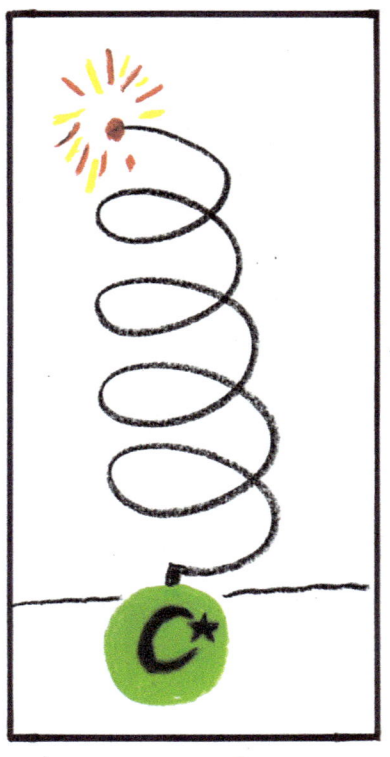

Arab Spring – a lot of Arabs killing each other. It saves us the trouble

Assimilated Jew – a Jew who acts like a goy in the street but has chicken soup with matzo balls for dinner

Atheism – a strict religion that preaches intolerance in the name of tolerance. Popular among progressive Jews

Auschwitz – currently, a hugely popular Jewish tourist destination

AZZ (Anti Zionist Zionists) – our controlled opposition apparatus

B

B, Zyklon – we prefer white phosphorus

Balfour Declaration – a sophisticated British plot designed to drag the USA into World War I

Barenboim, Daniel – a meshuggener gifted musician who loves peace and Wagner equally

Bat Mitzvah – the moment in time when Jewish parents celebrate the hope that their daughter may never see a foreskin

Bar Mitzvah – the moment when the male Jew accepts that his foreskin is not going to grow back

BBC – the Muslims say it is Islamophobic, we say it is anti-Semitic, all we know for sure is that they fiddle with kids

BDS, Ramallah Style – Barghouti, Diluted by Soros. Good for the Jews

BDS, Gaza Style – Ballistics, Determination & Strategy. Very bad for the Jews

BDS, Manhattan style – Benjamin, David & Samuel. They are the Jews

Ben Gurion – an airport near Tel Aviv

Bin Laden, Osama – a Jihadist Robin Hood. Good for the Jews

Blair, Tony – is not a Sabbath goy, he actually operates seven days a week; was still available at the time this book was published

Blood Diamond – one of the pillars of Israel's economy

Bolshevism – gave us a bad name for a while

Boycott – here is an ancient Jewish joke:
Q: How many synagogues do you need in a village with just one Jew?
A: Two. One for the Jew to go to, and one for him to boycott

Britain – the country that gave the world Shakespeare, the Beatles, Bertrand Russell and Ed Miliband

Brooks, Mel – what would it take for him to come up with 'spring time for Bibi and Tzipi?'

Bush, George W – more Zionist than Herzl, more horses than brain cells. Good for the Jews

C

Canaan – the land of milking money

Capitalism – just another 'ism' that elevates our symptoms into an ideology

Catch 22 – free ham

Charlie Hebdo – suicidal? Certainly! Funny?... meh, good for the Jews

China – a problem. A home for too many stubborn guiltless goyim who don't speak English, Yiddish or Hebrew

Chicken Soup – A.K.A Jewish penicillin - pretty effective for colds and flu, however, limited success rate for brain tumors, broken bones and white phosphorous wounds

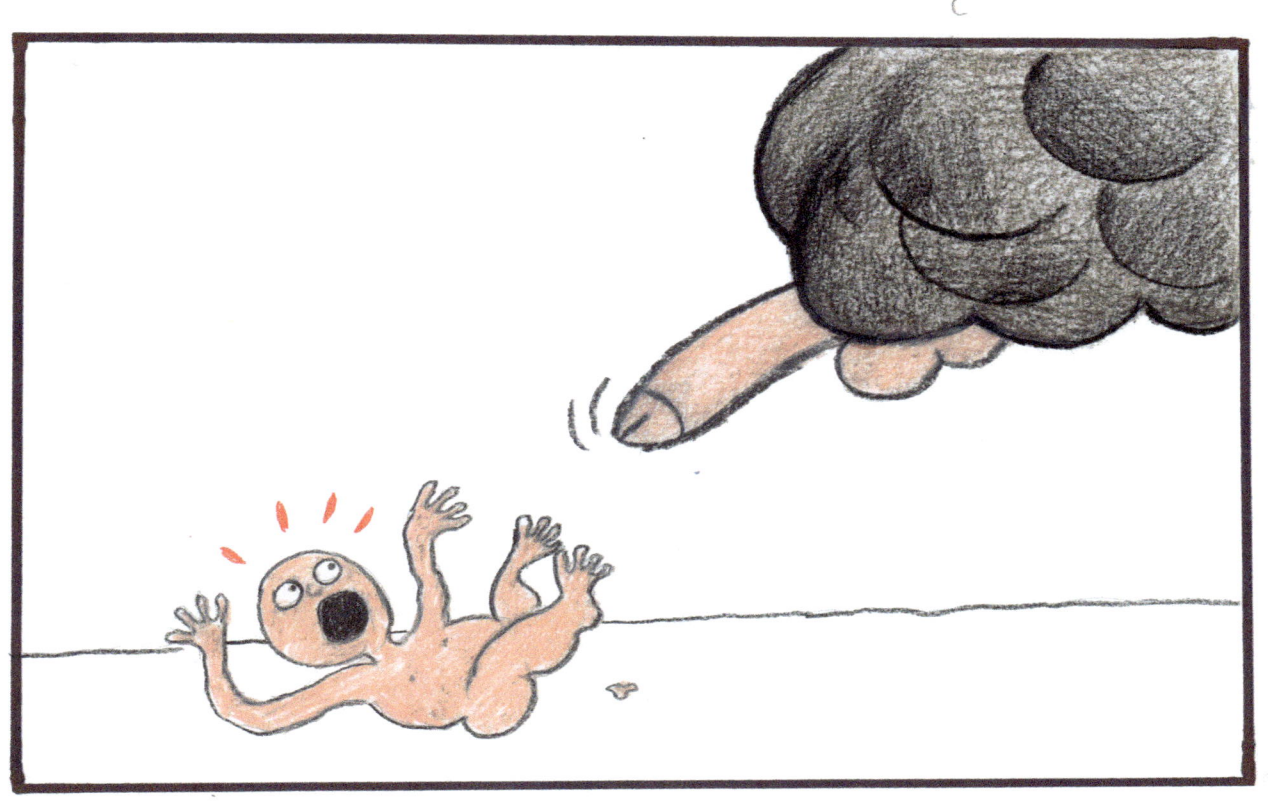

Children – a Jewish family's second most important asset

Chomsky, Noam – the Dershowitz of the anti Zionists

Chopped Liver – the Jewish answer to French pate

Christianity – was very bad for the Jews but now the danger is, somehow, contained

Christian Zionists – goyim who kill Muslims for Israel in the name of Jesus

Christmas – the goyim's answer to Hanukah

Circumcision (Brit Milah, Bris) – to cut a long story short. Jewish women won't buy unless there is 15% off. An ancient Jewish blood ritual also popular among progressive Jewish atheists and revolutionary Marxists

Circumcision, Female – popular in anti Zionist countries, it involves the removal of the clitoris. The mutilation has to be carried out by another female, as a man wouldn't be able to find it

Civilization – transforming the universe into an extended Tel Aviv

Clinton, Bill – he has shitty taste in women

Coca Cola – the fizzy form of American expansionism. Good for the Jews

Cohen, Sasha Baron – conspires to give anti-Semitism a bad name

Colonialism – a term popular with Jewish progressives. It makes the goyim believe that Israel is only as bad as Britain, Belgium and France (but 100 years later)

Communism – is how we teach the goyim to work as hard as possible and get as little as possible in return

Compassion – something we exhibit towards suffering people around the globe except our neighbours (who don't deserve us)

Concentration Camp – so we stay focused

Consensus – we all agree; Zionist, anti Zionist, Jews for Peace, Jews Against Cancer, Jews for Moral Intervention, Jews For Armageddon, Jews for Blue Cheese, the Jewish Chronicle, Chronically ill Jews, Jews for BBC Sex Victims: – Dieudonne, Mel Gibson and Atzmon are modern day Amalek

Cosmopolitan – an assimilated Jew who failed to integrate into any recognized non-Jewish group

D

David, Larry – the goyim find him funny because they believe his characters must be farfetched

Democracy – there is only one in the Middle East!

Demography – not good for the Jews!!!

Dershowitz, Alan – the Chomsky of the Zionists (though Chomsky is yet to be implicated in a sex scandal involving minors)

Deterrence, Power of – that which stops Israelis from returning to Sderot

Diaspora Jews – the innocent survivors of vile racist expulsion by the Romans. Have been living in exile in complete misery ever since

Dickens, Charles – an evil English man who invented Fagin many years before Bernie Madoff swallowed Elie Wiesel's savings

Dieudonné M'bala M'bala – the deluded French comedian who has failed to recognize the primacy of our suffering

Deir Yassin – viewing point for Yad Vashem

Dimona – a kosher nuclear bomb factory in southern Israel

Drones – so we can kill goyim from afar

E

Einstein, Albert – a relatively clever Jewish boy

Electronic Intifada – transformed Palestinian resistance into an internet blog. Good for the Jews

Equality – it makes us feel superior when we talk about it

Eurovision – the ideal platform to exhibit our broadminded approach toward gays, transgenders, ugly people, blacks and even Arabs

El Al – not to be confused with Halal

F

Fagin – not so good for the Jews

Falafel Balls – the testicles of a rare Biblical animal; a very special Jewish traditional dish adopted by the Arabs. Now popular in Palestine, Lebanon and Syria

Falashmura – black Jews from Ethiopia. They make good Israeli soldiers though we are still looking into the compatibility of their blood

False Flag – fools the goyim into believing that other goyim are particularly bad

Feminism – a Jew friendly identity politics front. Good for the Jews

Filipinos – were invented by God to replace the Palestinians

Finkelstein, Norman – the man who discovered the Holocaust Industry

Focused Assassination – the fate awaiting every authentic Palestinian

Foxman, Abe – a leading international humanist, interested solely in the suffering of one people, who happen to be us

Foreskin – no idea, never saw one

France – the country that gave the world Voltaire, Balzac and Bernard-Henri Levy

Frank, Anne – proves that we are ordinary, innocent people as well as faultless! Very good for the Jews

Frankfurt School – the definitive secular yeshiva

Friedman, Milton – the man who made service into 'economy' and egotism into a Western ideal

Friends of Israel – our lobby groups within the British Parliament (Labour, Conservative & Liberal Democrats), the manner by which we reduced Britain into an Israeli colony

G

G Spot – a sensitive point inside the female vagina. Named after Gilad Atzmon who is regarded as a cunt by all of us

Gays – we made our Tel Aviv into their capital so the goyim could see how liberal, tolerant and multicultural we are unlike our reactionary neighbours

Gatekeeper – a Jewish anti Zionist who burns books in the name of Palestine

Gaza – Palestinian Civilization Preservation Project – a sealed conservation area in the south of Israel where native Palestinians can cherish their culture and civilization in total isolation

Gefilte Fish – an Eastern European dish, a mixture of carp fish, old bread and leftovers. Not recommended for gentile consumption

Geller, Uri – proves that we can bend everything

Genocide – can other people have a Holocaust? You decide

Gentile – an inoffensive tag for the goy (basically, the rest of humanity)

Germans – are easily manipulated by guilt and make great cars

Ghetto – the physical, spiritual and practical embodiment of our inclination toward self-segregation

Gibson, Mel – a self loving goy, he must be destroyed

Global Zionism – puts world conflict into context

God – was invented by us so he could choose us over all other people

Golem – a kosher robot, e.g., Israeli drones, President Bush, etc.

Goy – an ordinary human being as opposed to a chosen one

Guilt – is something the goyim feel fairly often. Good for the Jews

Grass, Gunter – a goy who speaks out. Bad for the Jews

Greenspan, Alan – taught us how to fund Zionist global wars without diminishing Jewish wealth

Guantanamo Bay – a symptom of our success in Zionising the American legal system

Guardian, The – Jewish Chronicle for the goyim; The Guardian of Judea

Guardian Readers – people who read The Sun in secret

H

Haaretz – an Israeli daily paper, it conveys an image of Jewish decency. The goyim read it, Israelis don't

Hamas – a Palestinian homemade short-range rocket workshop. Not so good for the Jews

Hasbara – Israeli propaganda; our answer to Greek logic – it is simple, coherent, rational, consistent, totally deceitful and the goyim buy it

Hebrew – God's language, if we speak it we may as well be God

Herzl, Theodor – a visionary and charismatic bearded Jew who suddenly felt homesick after just 2000 years away. Not to be confused with Hertz car rental

Hezbollah – the ballistic sector within Shia Islam. Very bad for the Jews

Historian – a person who helps us to conceal our past

Hitler – He believed in chosenness

Hollywood – united against anti-Semitism, the savage and the Muslim. Very good for the Jews

Holocaust – when Jews are killed, a contemporary Western religion

Human Rights – a good pretext for global conflict

Human Shield – the manner in which our lobbies utilize western countries

Humus – a traditional Jewish Polish vegetarian dish brought to the Middle East by Zionist pioneers. Not to be confused with Hamas

Humour, Jewish – diverts attention from our problematic symptoms by means of self-deprecation

I

IDF – the most moral army in the world: it always thinks twice before it decides to kill civilians and it never forgets to apologize

Idiocy – misinterpreting goyim's tolerance as stupidity

Independent, The – it depends who you ask

International Law – who cares?

Intifada – when a bunch of Palestinian kids throw stones at an Israeli tank for more than 48 hours

Iran – a country populated by a lot of Shia Muslims who want to join the scientific revolution. Not good for the Jews

Iron Dome – the best Jewish invention since Yahweh (Jehovah)

Isis – they don't approve of the head and the body being attached

Islam – the religion of the people who live around our oil fields

Israeli – a person who suffers from acute occupational disorder

Israel – a place where we can punish Arabs for crimes committed by Europeans

Italians – the sons and the daughters of the murderers who nailed Jesus to the cross. It is about time Italy takes responsibility for murdering Christ

J

JAP (Jewish American Princess) – a punishment awaiting every American Jewish male

J Date – a Jewish dating website that attempts to counter the menace imposed by the Shikze (see also Shikze)

Jews – a concept that cannot be discussed openly.

Jewishness – the ideology of the above

Jewdaism (Judaism) – a religion most of the above discarded long ago

Jews, The – the people who give a bad name to the Jew

Jewish Question, The – "Will you take 20 quid?"

Jew, as a (as a Jew) – a common adage that silences the goyim (e.g., as a Jew I understand, as a Jew I insist, etc.)

Jewish Humor – the manner in which we admit our symptoms

Jewish Marxist – an oxymoron

Jewish non-profit organization – yeah, right!

Jewish Power – our unique capacity to silence opposition to Jewish power

Jewish Socialism – like National Socialism but kosher

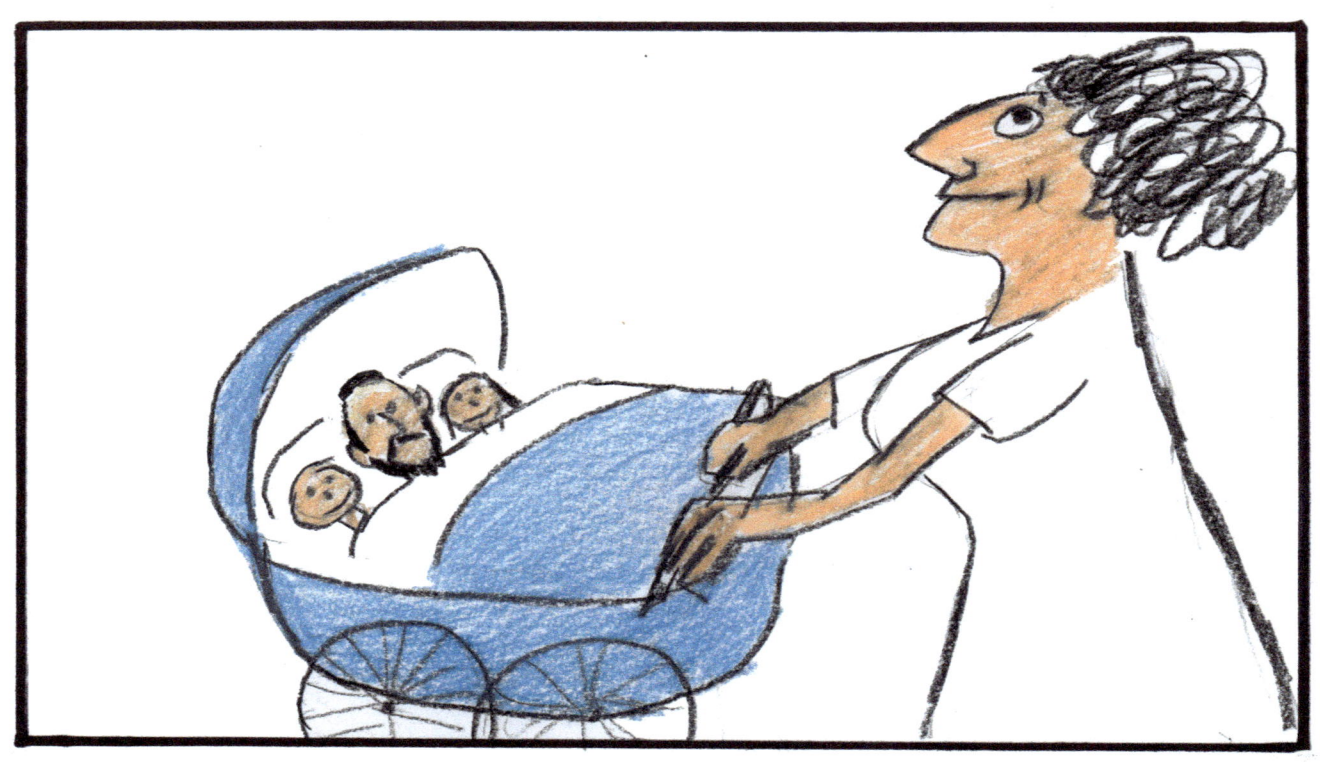

Jewish Mother – just like a Jewish father but with balls

Jesus – he wanted us to love our neighbours, funny

John Zorn – a New York, Jewish-American saxophone owner

J-Street – an American Jewish lobby that hunts down the very few politicians who escaped AIPAC (see also: AIPAC, Jewish Power, Soros)

Judeo-Christian – there is no such thing, but we better keep quiet about it

K

Kabbalah – makes Madonna look spiritual

Kibbutz – our attempt to form a Hebraic communal society. For some reason it didn't last very long

Kippa (skullcap, yarmulke) – the Jewish cure for baldness

Klezmer – gypsy music played so badly it became a new genre

Kissinger, Henry – a Jewish political scientist who made the planet his laboratory

Knesset – a safe haven for Israeli and diaspora Jewish criminals

Kosher – a set of Judaic dietary laws that guarantee zero assimilation and total segregation

L

Left, The – middle class people who know what is right for the working class. Good for the Jews

LGBT – Leah, Gershon, Benzion and Talya. Good for the Jews

Light Unto the Nations, A – white phosphorous in Gaza

Lord Goldsmith – the British Attorney General who gave Blair's government the green light to launch an illegal war against Iraq

Lewinsky, Monica – divine intervention: against all odds she managed to attract an American president. She must have studied The Book Of Esther closely

Lord Levy – chief fundraiser for the British Labour Government at the time Britain launched an illegal war against Iraq

Love Your Neighbor – an offensive and anti-Semitic suggestion that may lead to crucifixion (see also Italians)

M

Manhattan – the biggest kibbutz around – a few progressive, wonderful, democratic Jewish bankers surrounded by plenty of goyim 'volunteers'

Marx, Karl – the agitator Marxists never read, let alone understand

Marxist, A – a Godless orthodox Jew

Marx, Groucho – proof that we can also be funny for real

Masada – a kosher mass suicide, cherished by Israeli leaders, diaspora Jews in general and neocons in particular

Matzo – a tasteless cracker. Eaten by the Jews during Passover in commemoration of the pre-pita era

Media – the contemporary means of our intellectual, spiritual and political indoctrination

Mein Kampf – actually, our Kampf is bigger

Melanie Phillips – she must be cloned

Meshuggener – a person who looks for reason for no reason

Moral Intervention – a generic name for our expansionist wars

Mossad, The – a kosher search engine, a bunch of Jews who set off wars by way of deception and believe no one notices

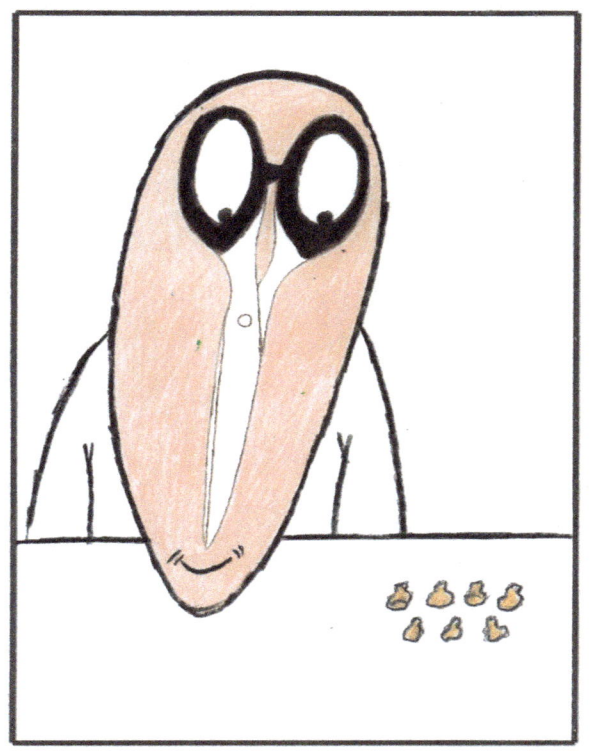

Mohel – a Jew who chops foreskins for a living

Muslims – people who refuse to believe in Coca Cola. For some peculiar reason they prefer Allah

Muslim Brotherhood – is what happens when you let Arabs have a true democracy

N

911 – a nice German sports car

Nakba – a moment in time when Palestinians voluntarily decided to give their homes and land to European Jewish pioneers. Later they changed their minds

Natural Death – not very common in Gaza

Nazism – Nationalist, Racist and Expansionist but unlike Zionism, it didn't last long

Neoconservatism – the shift from a 'promised land' to a 'promised planet'

Netanyahu, Benjamin (Bibi) – he speaks good American English and he looks better than Ahmadinejad

New Testament – slightly too naïve for a canonical spiritual book

NGO – a system designed to neutralize rising dissent and young Palestinian leadership (see also George Soros)

O

Obama, Barack – holds the Guinness world record for the 'shortest lasting greatest hope'

Oil – a lubricant the Arabs are happy to give away but Anglo Americans prefer to plunder

Old Testament – more violent than Tarantino's films

Oligarchs, Russian – people who convert Russian wealth into shekels

Olive Oil – a greasy lubricant Palestinian solidarity activists sell at their miniature political gatherings

Olive Tree – a plant that plays an essential role in the Palestinian economy. It lives forever. Occasionally relocated to posh Israeli gardens, it makes its new owners feel like an integral part of the region and its history

Open Society Institute – a charity dedicated to the transformation of deprived people into Guardian readers (see also George Soros)

Operations (Pillar of Edge, Cloud of Lead, Protective Cast, etc.) – extensive attempts to examine the impact of white phosphorous and uranium depleted shells on human flesh

Organ Trafficking – a respectable way of making a living by saving other people's lives

Orientalists - people who say things Arabs prefer to deny

Oslo Accord – a window of political opportunists

Oy Vey – a popular Jewish expression often uttered following a colossal tragic event such as a pogrom or slipping on a banana skin

P

Palestinians – a uniquely stubborn breed of Arab who, for some peculiar reason, chose to live in our promised homeland

PA (Palestinian Authority) – Palaestinensischer Judenrat

Peace – a good reason for a war

Peres, Shimon – as clever as a rabbi, as shrewd as a Rothschild and as honest as Bernie Madoff

Palestinian Flag (colours) – green for cucumber, red for tomato, white for peace and black for the future

Pig – the most precious animal in the Jewish universe. We don't eat it, we don't farm it, we just let it be

PLO – Paralysed Liberation Organisation

Pogrom – when the goyim surrender to their savage inclinations. Very bad for the Jews

Political Correctness – a political stand that doesn't allow political criticism. Very good for the Jews

Political Zionism – the transformation of super powers into our mercenaries

Post Modernism – telling the goyim that the truth is complex in case they hadn't noticed

Post Structuralism – dismantling all grand narratives except the Jewish one

Post Traumatic Bris Disorder – the life of the Jewish male, often inflicted on the Jewish female

Post Traumatic Stress Disorder – the state of being tormented by someone else's past

Pre Traumatic Stress Disorder – the state of being traumatised by an imaginary future event

Post Zionism – telling the Palestinians that they were ethnically cleansed in case they didn't know

Progressive – an inoffensive label for Judeo-centric activism within the left

Promised Land – the transformation of the Bible into a property deed and God into a real estate agent

Protocols Of The Elders Of Zion – diverts goyim's attention from our overwhelming influence in politics, media, culture and finance by an endless debate over the authenticity of an anti-Semitic Tsarist forgery

PSC (Palestinian Solidarity Campaign) – a home for British dysfunctional Trotskyites, retired minor union activists and elder anti Zionist Zionists. Good for the Jews

Qassam Rockets – a ballistic weapon designed to hit hard on open areas surrounding Israeli cities

Quenelle – an anti establishment salute invented by the French comedian, Dieudonne Mbla Mbla. We find it very upsetting, probably because we view ourselves as the establishment

Quran – a problem, it is still more popular than Harry Potter, let alone Anne Frank

Quartet, The – provides Tony Blair with a diplomatic title and a safe haven in Israel

R

Rabbi – a Jewish religious scholar who knows the Talmud well enough to keep it to himself

Ramallah – Palestinian NGO capital

Racism – is when the goy starts to think and behave like us

Revisionism, History – an attempt to grasp what really happened. Not good for the Jews

Reactionary – an idea that doesn't fit our correct vision of the world

Relief & Aid – how the West turns proud nations into a bunch of beggars

Right Wing – a goy who thinks like an Israeli

Right of Return – the undeniable obligation of every Jew to settle in Zion

Robert Allen Zimmerman – (Shabtai Zisel ben Avraham), is what Bob Dylan was named at his bris. Unlike Stevie Wonder, Zimmerman still plays in Tel Aviv

Rothschild – is what world banking is all about. Certainly good for the Rothschilds

Rubber Bullets – another example of Jewish genius

Russia – the country that gave the world Dostoyevsky, Tolstoy, Anatoly Sheransky and Roman Abramovich

Sabbath – no traffic jam in Golders Green

Sabbath Goy – a goy who toadies to our whims

Sabra – the Palestinian name for the prickly pear fruit, reminiscent of Palestinian civilisation on our promised land

Sabra – an Israeli born Jew. Like the prickly pear above, the Sabra is tough and thorny on the outside but unlike the diaspora Jew is thought to be genuine, soft and sweet on the inside

Said, Edward W – Barenboim's friend

Samaritan, The Good – the archetypal good goy

Sayan – (Israeli assistant) a diaspora Jew who loves his people more than his neighbours

Selfish – is actually kosher unlike shellfish

Self Hater – a person who loves himself hating himself

Self Hating Jew – what... there's another kind?

Settler – an Israeli Jew

Shakespeare, William – introduced us to organ trafficking

Sharon, Ariel – Israel's best soldier, also remembered as our longest lasting vegetable

Separation Wall – so the world is isolated

Settlements – the reason why there is no lasting settlement

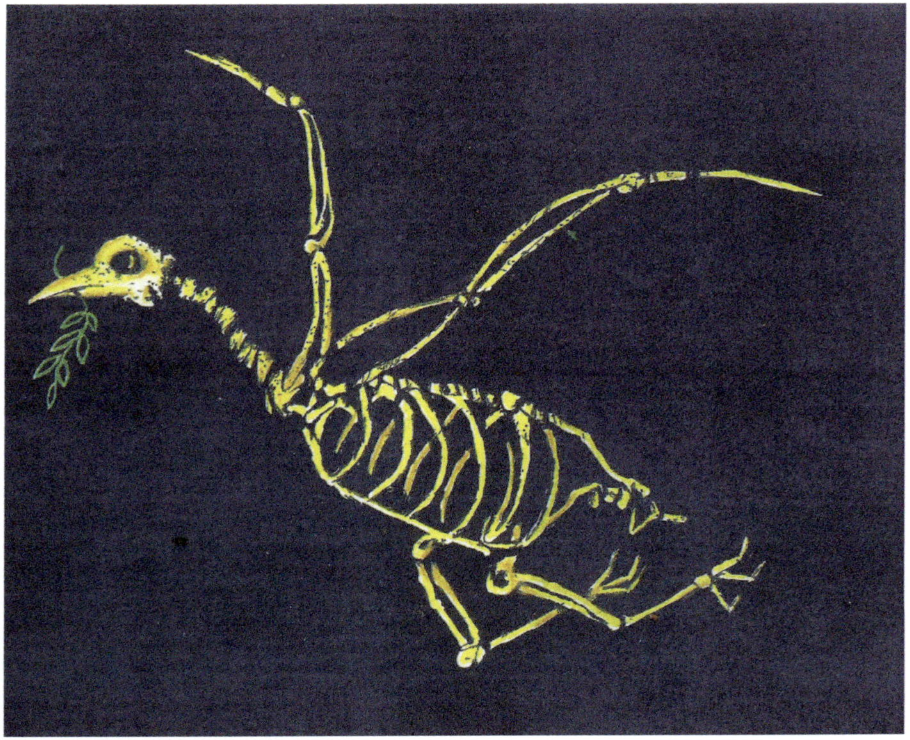

Shalom – means security for the Jews. Not to be confused with peace or reconciliation

Shekel – without us producing a single thing, our currency is somehow stronger than the British Pound, more attractive than the US Dollar, more solid than the Euro. Must be divine intervention

Shikze – gentile female, the Jewish male's ultimate object of desire. Also, 'the ultimate threat' as far as the Jewish mother is concerned

Shoa – traditionally refers to the Nazi Judeocide; it can also refer to minor incidents involving Jewish interests

Shoa Business – attaching a barcode to our suffering

Shoes – the means by which Muslims express their political dissent

Shoes, pile of – maintains the goyim's guilt

Sieg Heil – an inverted quenelle

Six Day War – (two hours more likely) the moment in history when we realised that the IDF was even greater than God

Soros, George – a liberal Zionist who funds a lot of good causes (see NGO) that are also very good for the Jews

Solution, One State, Two State, No State – a bunch of opinionated diaspora Jews trying to tell us how to live

Spanish Civil War – an opportunity to kill a few Catholics and burn their churches, all in the name of the proletariat revolution

Spinoza, Baruch – name of a street in Tel Aviv

Spielberg, Steven – the man behind E.T, a cinematic tale of an alien who lost his way back to the ghetto but managed to befriend a few goyim for almost two hours

Stalin - the person who killed Trotsky (and 20,000,000 anonymous goyim)

Starbucks Coffee – the goyim need their latte and the shikzes need their skinny cappuccino

Star of David – a symbol of Nazi discrimination (when yellow) and Israeli omnipotence (when blue & white)

Suicide Bomber – a wealthy and spoiled rich young Palestinian motivated solely by irrational hatred against innocent Jews choosing martyrdom for no reason

T

3rd & 4th Generation – young Israelis who believe themselves to be traumatized by other people's suffering

Tallit – the Jewish male's answer to the Burka

Talmud – the spiritual DNA of Jewish self love

Tel Aviv – the mecca of Jewish escapism

Ten Commandments, The – reminds us that murdering is not nice and stealing can also upset others

Terror – the fear that a democratically elected government may send people (dressed as Muslims) to kill you

Tear Gas – the IDF's onion

Terrorist – how we label Muslims

Time – we buy

Tikkun Olam – conveys the false image that we know how to fix the world

Torah – makes us believe that we have a collective beginning

Trotskyism – the most advanced form of kosher Bolshevism

Tunnels – the Palestinian answer to our air superiority

U

UN – a lot of resolutions, nice blue hats

Universalism – a strange idea that suggests that people have something in common

USA – the country that gave us John Coltrane and Bin Laden

Uranium Depleted Shells – modern artillery is our method of getting rid of our nuclear waste

V

Volvo – British Jews' favorite car. It is big, drives like a tank, it is amphibious and it isn't German

Vanunu, Mordechai – Jews better play the fiddle rather than blow the whistle

Wandering Jew, The – a person who is detached from land, nature and neighbors, e.g. the Israeli

Wagner – wasn't asked to compose the Israeli anthem

Water – is vital for all known forms of life except Palestinians

Washington – our most powerful colony

Wailing Wall, The – because talking to God is like talking to a brick wall

War Against Terror – we won

West Bank, The – just like other banks it costs the American taxpayers a lot of money

Wolfowitz, Paul – the man who helped transform America into an Israeli mission force

Women – unlike our reactionary neighbours, we treat them as if they are equal

Women's Rights – a fabulous excuse to kill Muslims. Good for the Jews

World Zionist Congress – the kosher Illuminati

Xenophobia – pretty much like anti-Semitism but universal

Y

Yad Vashem – must be an important place because every world leader is photographed there

Yassin, Sheikh Hammed – a legendary Palestinian leader and founder of the Hamas. Proved to be fatally vulnerable to missiles

Yiddish - just to make sure we are indecipherable to the goyim

Yom Kippur War (1973) – is when we lost our confidence for 48 hours

Z

Zahal (Israeli Military Service) – What young Israelis do before moving furniture in New York

Zelig – we appear in many shapes, forms and voices. We are simultaneously progressive and reactionary, capitalist and Bolshevik, Zionist and 'anti', we support wars and oppose them and we get away with it (most of the time)

Zionist Theory – doesn't work in practice

Zionist – a person who loves himself loving himself loving his people loving themselves. Not necessarily good for the Jews

Zionism – a false promise to take the diaspora Jews away and to give the goyim a break

Just to thank all the great people who helped us to form this extensive lexicon. The Atzmon family; Mai and Yann, Aaron Barshak (comedy terrorist) who contributed some of the best entries, Eve Mykytyn for the extensive editorial support, Yossi Goldin (Yos), Cl. Daphna Abramovitch (Daph), Lt Gen Gabi Cohen (Gabko) and Brig Gen Moshe Levi (Mushiko), for the spiritual support, Alan Dershowitz (Sayan 007) and Abe'le Foxman for being themselves.

We would love to express our admiration and love to the entire chosen people, the Jewish State, IDF and the Mossad and also to pay respect to The Left, the Miliband family and the entire network of Goyim who look after our interests and have supported us all along.

Never again (hopefully)

GILAD & ENZO

MY LEXICON

THIS SPACE IS FOR YOU TO MAKE UP YOUR OWN